Packed and Loaded

Selected Conversations Between

James M. Cain

And

Edgar Allan Poe Award Winner John McAleer

Afterword By Shamus Award Winner Jeremiah Healy

Compiled By Harry Sapienza And Andrew McAleer

Nimble Books LLC

Nimble Books LLC

1521 Martha Avenue

Ann Arbor, MI, USA 48103

http://www.NimbleBooks.com

wfz@nimblebooks.com

+1.734-330-2593

Version 1.0; last saved 2010-05-27.

Printed in the United States of America

ISBN-13: 978-1-60888-047-8

∞ The paper used in this publication meets the minimum requirements of the American National Standard for Information Sciences—Permanence of Paper for Printed Library Materials, ANSI Z39.48-1992. The paper is acid-free and lignin-free.

CONTENTS

ABOUT *PACKED AND LOADED*

In 1975 James M. Cain commissioned Dr. McAleer to write his biography and, before Cain died in 1977, McAleer seized every possible opportunity to interview Cain on his life, craft, and peers. In these never-before-published interviews, Cain discusses his first notions to be a writer, his newspaper days, his Hollywood years, and Marilyn Monroe with brutal honesty and in a tone and vernacular that only a master like Cain could command. Also in this critical, tell-it-like-it-is study, Cain reveals his thoughts on Hemingway, Fitzgerald, Arthur Miller, Hammett, Chandler, and, in his eighty-fifth year, what he planned for his future. For more than three decades these interviews were believed lost, until the summer of 2001, when Professor McAleer discovered them co-habiting with his P.G. Wodehouse correspondence (in a relationship as fortuitous as it was seemingly incongruous). *Packed and Loaded* is James M. Cain "unplugged", at his finest. The manuscript is seasoned with original epigraphs about this major American writer from masters like Elmore Leonard, Sue Grafton, Robert B. Parker, Dennis Lehane, Peter Lovesey, Phil Lovesey, Edward D. Hoch, Katherine Hall Page, Robin Moore, William G. Tapply, and the grand master of mystery himself, Rex Stout.

ABOUT JOHN MCALEER

John McAleer graduated from Harvard University with a Ph.D. in English Literature and was the author of over a dozen books, including an Edgar Award-winning biography of Rex Stout. He was nominated for the Pulitzer Prize for his biography of Emerson. He wrote critically-acclaimed studies of Thoreau and Dreiser, as well as a definitive novel on the Korean War, *Unit Pride.* The Washington Post compared his mystery novel, *Coign of Vantage,* to the works of Oscar Wilde, Evelyn Waugh, and Lewis Carroll. A Bostonian and a professor of English at Harvard and then Boston College for more than half a century, Dr. McAleer lived in Massachusetts with his wife Ruth and Labrador, Shadow. At the time of his death in November 2003, he was completing a definitive biography of Jane Austen. His book, *Mystery Writing in a Nutshell*, co-authored with his son Andrew McAleer, became a number 1 best seller posthumously.

ABOUT ANDREW MCALEER

Andrew McAleer is the author of *The 101 Habits of Highly Successful Novelists* and the co-author of the number 1 best seller *Mystery Writing in a Nutshell.* He is also the author of three crime novels including the well-received *Double Endorsement* and *Bait and Switch.* Mr. McAleer works as a prosecutor and teaches at Boston College. He serves as a Specialist with the Army National Guard.

PRAISE FOR JOHN MCALEER ...

"A worthy effort in every respect ... [John McAleer] does his subject justice—Fine research, a clear judicious eye, a keen critical sense, a felicitous style ... there's never a dull moment in his perceptive opus."

—*Publishers Weekly*

"The definitive account by a master biographer."

—*Jacques Barzun & Wendell Hertig Taylor*
A Catalogue of Crime

"This is a superb book ... All friends of Rex Stout, Nero Wolfe, and Archie Goodwin are in John McAleer's debt."

—*Norman Cousins*
Saturday Review of Literature

"John McAleer ... portrays a life every bit as engrossing as a Nero Wolfe mystery. The full flavor of Stout's wit and urbanity comes through."

—*Lawrence Meyer*
Washington Post

"Coming generations of readers will hold McAleer's name in respect for the very thoroughness with which he has met his responsibilities as authorized biographer."

—*John Wintermeyer, Q.C.*
The Ontario Globe

"Easily the finest biography of a mystery writer since the late John Dickson Carr's superb 1949 life of Conan Doyle."

—*Edgar Award winner Francis M. Nevins, Jr.*
St. Louis Globe

FOREWORD

During the 70s, when James M. Cain decided that the long silence of his designated biographer, Roy Hoopes, signified Hoopes's permanent loss of interest with the project, he asked me, an established figure in the field of literary biography, to write his biography.

Over a two-year period I compiled a stack of interviews with Cain. Then Hoopes resurfaced. To spare Cain his blushes I yielded ground to Hoopes but, while concealing my pique well enough to receive an acknowledgement of his indebtedness from Hoopes when his life of Cain appeared five years after the subject's demise, I retained, in their entirety, my own interviews.

In the summer of 2001 my son Andrew discovered these never-before-published Cain interviews and Cain's only known works of poetry co-habiting with my P.G. Wodehouse correspondence. For the past two years Andrew and I have been bestowing order on Cain's perceptive, uninhibited, reflections. These reflections reveal Cain as he wanted to be remembered. There never was a time when Cain was not forthright in utterance, but in his octogenarian interviews age sanctioned an awareness remote from the restraints wariness might have imposed on a lesser mortal, a decade earlier. At eighty-five he dared to give free expression to an estimate of his fellow man with an integrity, which even those less engaged in reality would scorn to rebuke.

John McAleer, Ph.D.
Professor of English, Boston College
Permanent Fellow, Durham University (England)
Webster Island, Duxbury, Massachusetts

INTRODUCTION

It is Rex Stout who deserves the credit for introducing me to James M. Cain, and while I'm not so sure the postman does actually ring twice—or even once for that matter—I know now that Rex Stout indeed does.

In May of 1978, my father returned home from the Mystery Writers of America's annual dinner in New York City with a new member of the family—Edgar Allan Poe. By unanimous vote, his *Rex Stout: A Biography* (now *Rex Stout: A Majesty's Life* with James A. Rock & Company Publishers) won the Edgar Allan Poe award for critical works.

Prior to Stout, my father had established himself in the field of literary biography having authored major works on Thoreau and Dreiser, but it was ultimately Stout that would garner him praise from literary giants like Jacques Barzun who hailed him as " ... a master biographer." And Norman Cousins—whose high standards are a matter of record—of the *Saturday Review of Literature* said of *Stout* "This is a superb book .... All friends of Rex Stout, Nero Wolfe, and Archie Goodwin are in John McAleer's debt." It wasn't until many years later—during law school in fact—that I would become a friend of Wolfe and Archie; and therefore, be in my father's literary debt.

To help maintain what little sanity I had left in law school, I devoured Stouts and not just the Wolfe stories.

I breezed through novels like *The Mountain Cat*, *The Hand in the Glove*, his pulp stories collected in *Justice Ends at Home*, and I'll even admit to reading *Alphabet Hicks*—who Stout himself said he wouldn't give a damn for. I also read my father's biography on Stout and its companion, *Royal Decree: Conversations with Rex Stout*. In the chapter, "Rex on His Peers," I came across this quote from Stout:

> I think Cain's a hell of a good storyteller, a marvelous storyteller. That way of telling a story—I don't think you can do it any better than *The Postman Always Rings Twice*. It can't be done better than that. I think it's a perfect job. If I were asked to name the living writer who I think has stuck most closely to that idea—stick to the story, stick to the goddamn story—it probably would be James M. Cain. There's not a word in Cain that does not apply to the story he's telling you.

This was the first ring. As a new author I took Stout's words to heart and read *The Postman Always Rings Twice* and would quickly move on to *Double Indemnity*, *The Butterfly*, *The Embezzler*, and *Career in C Major*. Not that I ever had any doubts, but Stout couldn't have been more right about Cain and his ability to stick to the story. Simple advice that might be easy to understand, but difficult to put into action.

I took Cain to heart and wanted to learn more about him, so I asked my father what would be the definitive biography on Cain. Without missing a beat he suggested Roy Hoopes's biography and then, almost casually, he said that his notes on Cain might also be helpful. "What do you mean?" I asked. And then he told me that during the 1970s, Cain had asked him to write his biography. My father lamented, however, that the notes were probably long gone, but that I was welcomed to rifle his files. I looked under "C" no luck. Under "J" no luck. Under "M" no luck. And since my father's files are voluminous, containing more than a half century's worth of research from Jane Austen, to Sir Arthur Conan Doyle to Patrick O'Brian, I knew I'd have as much luck finding the misplaced Cain papers as I would a Bible at a tax planning seminar. Thankfully, Stout was not so pessimistic.

The doorbell rang again. It was around this time that a publisher sought permission to reprint the Stout Biography with an updated Introduction. P.G. Wodehouse wrote the Foreword to the original Biography and my father thought it might be nice to review his correspondence with Wodehouse to see if he could come up with any new tidbits for the new Stout Introduction. I told him I'd fetch them for him and when I returned with the file, I carried with me a sheaf of Cain material.

Now in my hands were original Cain envelopes containing original letters with extensive marginalia from Cain's own hand. Also contained were my father's interviews, typed out nearly a quarter of a century ago on his IBM electric, which sits in my office today. Some of the interviews were compiled via correspondence and some by tape recorder, recorded by one of my father's top-notch graduate students at Boston College, Harry Sapienza.

Harry lived near Cain in Maryland, so my father arranged for them to visit during the Thanksgiving break of 1976. Armed with pages upon pages full of questions drafted by father, young Harry met with Cain and did a remarkable job of getting Cain to record his thoughts. Fortunately, the recordings had been transcribed before their disappearance —coincidentally, their disappearance occurred around the time Poe appeared on the scene! (Well, that's our convenient excuse.)

The Cain tapes have not yet surfaced, but I haven't given up hope—not by a long shot. I have great faith that the presence of Rex Stout and James M. Cain ring eternal.

Andrew McAleer
McGuinn Hall
Boston College

CHAPTER I. CAIN ON HIS CRAFT

"Cain's work has been considered the high-point of prose writing—specifically because of his control of the hard-bitten, no-nonsense argot of the American Depression that even now simply leaps off the page at the reader. Cain worked in the action-suspense field of the crime thriller, and helped set the tone for what is now called the voguish 'film noir.'"

—*The Literature of Crime and Detection*

"What I gained from reading Cain is an appreciation of the antagonist's point of view: that bad guys are more fun to write about than good guys, their attitude and they way they talk always more entertaining."

—*Elmore Leonard*

McAleer:[1] How long have you lived in Maryland?

James M. Cain: I lived here between seven or eight years, in this house. I used to, before that I lived in California, and before that New York, and before that, Baltimore.

McAleer: Have the places you lived influenced your writing?

[1] As noted in the Foreword, John McAleer's graduate student Harry Sapienza, who lived near Cain's home in Maryland, read McAleer's questions to Cain.

JMC: I was not just imagining stuff out of the whole cloth. In this book called *Rainbow's End*, I went up to Marietta, Ohio, for that book, because I wanted this hijacker to come down with this girl wrapped around him on this island. But it had to be an island in the river. And I had run into this river covering a story ...

McAleer: A story?

JMC: What was I doing? ... Out there? I was on a story that later became a story about the Red River expedition. The title of it was *Mio.* I wanted to be thorough, though, about my knowledge of the Mississippi River. When I started up there at Parkersburg, and I wanted some dope on Watahasett's Island, which I took a charter boat to run down to from Parkersburg, and then, also I got very caught up by the River Museum at Marietta. So I know this country fairly well, and this book, *Rainbow's End,* I put up the Maskinga River from Marietta and went up there to mostly as a question of covering the terrain and a little bit on the kind of people that lived alongside the river. But it did not much. It was also about mountain people that came over and lived there. The book came off all right. It suffered in one way from an ending I never made quite as good as I should have made it. But I had that happen with *Mildred Pierce,* too. The end of *Mildred Pierce* always was faulty. I did all right but ...

What else you got?

McAleer: Did you ever try to write any poetry?

JMC: I wrote two poems in my life. One came out in this paper I edited over in France, *The Lorraine Cross.* I was editor-in-chief of the division newspaper, and this was it:

> This talk of mother's cooking is very fine I grant,
> But there is just one other thing I want to have and can't.
> It's Charles's golden wheat cakes I long to taste anew,
> Those dear old standard wheat cakes, all plastered up with goo.

Now that's one poem I wrote, in my life. The other poem I put every time I send my contribution to a girl that's getting married. I put in there:

> Happy marriage.
> Original poem by Mister James M. Cain.
>
> In one respect all brides are alike and they don't think it funny.
> Whatever you give this blushing bunch they'd rather have the money.

So those are my two poems. That subject is quickly and easily covered. Definitively. No other poems I ever wrote in my life.

McAleer: Do you think that your experience as a journalist helped you with writing fiction?

JMC: I don't think it helped much. I don't think they have much relationship. I heard a man talk about the newspaper business and said I've done these imagined books and factory in the newspaper ... that he could say what he wanted to say—and I don't quite know what that means. Actually, the newspaper business does not help you write novels, I don't think. I suppose, in the newspaper business does have an effect on your style. But maybe not too much at that. In my novels, I don't write the way I write for a newspaper at all. Writing editorials for Lippmann, which was my best newspaper work, I wrote with a somewhat phony "don't-quite-take-it-too-seriously," I think it's more of a burlesque about elegance than the thing itself. It was quite part of my psychological nature, my nature, that I could pretend to be the corporate awfulness of the newspaper. That suited me fine, and I don't know that any part of that ever got into my novels. To write a novel, I have to pretend to be somebody else. I have to be, pretend to be, the character telling his story.

McAleer: Some of your novels are in the third person, however.

JMC: I wrote three books in the third person: *Mildred Pierce*, *Love's Lovely Counterfeit*, and *The Magician's Wife*. And, it tells a story, I seem to be able to get away with it but not with any such impact and conviction and circumstantial, background, as I get when I have the character tell the story. Now then, there's this also—maybe I'm inventing reasons for doing this first-personal narrative way, not third person. In the first person it seemed as though it really happened. Now, E.B. White, who's not easy to fool, wrote me a note when I had this story come out called "The Baby in the Icebox." About a guy that kept a roadside zoo—that's something that, they do out in California—to attract trade to his lunchroom. People stop in to look at the bear, and they buy a sandwich, and a bottle of beer. And he got really ambitious and put a tiger in. The tiger almost killed him one day. But the wife, to her, she was just a rejected cat, and she'd go in and feed the tiger and she and the tiger got to be real pals. And then—he knew nothing about this, and figured a way of getting her killed by the tiger. And that was the story. Well, E.B. White wrote me, when the story came out in *The American Mercury*, to know if the thing really happened, it seemed so real to him. And, as I say, E.B. White, he's a twenty-minute egg, he's not easy to fool. It seems as though it really happened when you read it. In the third person, I don't care how good you are, or even if you're Sinclair Lewis, there come times when it seems as though you're making up, making it up as you go along. To that extent, first-personal narration must be respected. It has its limitations, and yet it always steps up things. I spend more time figuring why the character should be telling this fantastic thing, I have to figure that one out: what's he telling this for? In *The Postman Always Rings Twice,* it seemed simple enough, he was, he had to die, and he wanted to leave some record of this love story between him and Cora, this girl who had helped him knock off her husband, and it all seemed so wonderful and beautiful. It seemed perfectly in character and plausible that he would be telling this story in a death house. For example, in *The Moth*, there didn't seem to be any good reason that this fellow would be telling the story, but he did tell it. I invented some reason that he'd be telling it—I've forgotten what it was. Especially when they had to write it—now that they have to tape it, you can believe it better, because it's not anything like as physical labor to tape as it is to write. They have someone type, or type it.

McAleer: Do you think the reading audience has changed much? When I read *Serenade* and *The Postman Always Rings Twice*, the narrators were characters who were very American and had definite ethnic prejudices. Do you think today's readers might be too sensitive about such a narrator?

JMC: Oh, I don't think so, because after all, because it doesn't say that I have any ethnic prejudice, it says the character. I think in this personal book *[The Postman Always Rings Twice]* he kept talking about the Greek, as though, "How could you marry this Greek?" he asked her, as though a Greek wasn't much to be married to. And she said, "Is that any of your business?" "Yeah," he said, "plenty." And he knew that she was kind of sensitive about it, but if she was sensitive about it she was ethnically prejudiced, and so was he. But it seemed to me that the reader would simply accept that's how they were and not particularly think I had to be—or assume that I had no right to mention it. I think this ethnic thing is carried much too far. I mean, it's there, why can't a novelist mention it?

McAleer: You spoke about stories being retold, such as *Vanity Fair* and so forth. Do you object to a good story being reworked? Do you have feelings about plagiarism?

JMC: Wait a minute. Which? Like which stories?

McAleer: Well, I'm not talking about any in particular.

JMC: If you're not talking about any in particular I can't answer you.

McAleer: Well, for example, in medieval times they didn't mind retelling a story, telling it in many different ways, having a lot of analogues, and ....

JMC: What's an analogue?

McAleer: Shakespeare, for example, may have based "Romeo and Juliet" on another play, that has the same basic plot, that's an analogue to his plot. That he has taken in, because he either saw something in the plot that he wanted to rework or he just liked the story so much that he just wanted to tell it in another way.

JMC: And what's your question?

McAleer: My question is how you feel about that sort of thing?

JMC: I don't have no feelings about it. It's not part of my thinking. To give you an answer would be just adlibbing something, no additional greater meaning to it. It's not a question I have convictions about one way or the other. I just don't think about it.

McAleer: Do some episodes in your books please you or stand out more that others?

JMC: Once the book is written, I never think about the goddamn book anymore. I get on with the next book.

McAleer: Have any authors influenced you greatly?

JMC: The only author that had any real influence on me was Lardner. Ring Lardner. Not the young Lardner whom I used to know pleasantly enough in Hollywood, but the elder Ring Lardner. And my brother and I both read with such delight these stories. They would come out in the *Saturday Evening Post*. "You know me, Al." Do you know Lardner?

McAleer: No.

JMC: Well, everybody was saying, "You know me, Al," and this girl over in Chestertown would say ... she'd say—try to be up to date—"You know Al!" [Laughter, Cain] Didn't make any sense. But Vincent and I, and my mother and I, when he got in the Marine Corps, where he was finally killed in a plane accident, and I, in France, would write each other "You know me, Al" letters, and ah, to that extent I had to go through the motions of imitating Lardner. And there may be some trace of Lardner in these early dialogues that I wrote for *The American Mercury,* that came out in a book called *Our Government.* And these dialogues all purported to tell how government was carried on in the United States. I don't think it's quite carried on that way but they made a couple of hours' funny reading and, ah, we hope it was funny. The book did have more than one edition so we didn't do too badly. And, oh, that's the only influence of writing that I have any consciousness of.

McAleer: Do you think creative writing can be taught?

JMC: No.

McAleer: Are you first or most attracted to the characters or central characters or to the story you want to tell?

JMC: I can't answer that. I don't know. Actually I don't know, and I doubt if any writer knows.

McAleer: When you're writing do you consciously set limits on what a writer should say or could say in a book?

JMC: That has no meaning for me. I don't set any limits. I never heard of a writer that sets limits on what a writer can say.

McAleer: You sometimes use a little profanity.

JMC: A little profanity. Sometimes if I need a "hell" or a "goddamn" I put it in, but it's like garlic: a little bit goes a long way. And once I use one of them, I'm done with it. And the four-letter words. I think I did use a four-letter word in *The Institute*, where I more or less had to. And in *Mildred Pierce* I used a four-letter word. He said something like she was a "beautiful piece of tail." But mostly, I lay off it.

McAleer: What do you want to be remembered for?

JMC: I don't know. It's just an idea that never enters my mind. It's a question I have no answer for. There's nothing that sticks in my mind, comes to mind that I would, could answer that question. What else you got there?

CHAPTER 2. CAIN ON HIS PEERS

> "In many ways James M. Cain set the standard for pacing, tightness of plot, and psychological suspense. *The Postman Always Rings Twice, The Butterfly, Double Indemnity*—to name just a few of his novels—rank foremost in the field of crime literature."
>
> —*Robin Moore*

McAleer: Did you ever meet Hemingway?

JMC: No. I never met Hemingway. Everybody, when he was out to Hollywood, in connection with raising money or selling bonds or whatever it was for the Spanish Loyalists, wanted to take me down to meet Hemingway. But I never wanted to meet him. I didn't really think that I'd like him. And one reason that I wouldn't meet him was that I knew I would never call him " *Papa*." And told myself, "I guess I'd be goddamned if I did that refrain. And if you didn't call him " *Papa*," I don't think he liked you too well. So rather than have this issue come up, I had very little if any curiosity to meet Hemingway. I don't know—I didn't—there's something about what I read about him and heard about him that didn't attract me personally. Ah, there's some of them dead, like Thornton Wilder, who I knew fairly well, but there's something about this guy that are so warm and likeable I knew before I met him that I was going to like him, if I ever did meet him and I did. And Red Lewis made himself very agreeable to me, and I knew him fairly well. And you so seldom saw him sober that you couldn't really make up your mind whether you really liked him or more or less dreaded him. But you couldn't disregard the tremendous things this guy did. Doggonit, you knew that you had to respect him anyhow. And underneath this drunken guy there was always one or two women, too. *Make Like Funny With The Man Who Knew Coolidge*—Christ, I heard him recite this thing fifty times before he ever put it out as a book. Well, what's the rest of it? What else you got?

McAleer: Do you have any opinion of Jane Austen?

JMC: Jane Austen? I never read one word by Jane Austen.

McAleer: How would you rank Hammett and Chandler as hard-boiled authors?

JMC: I've been accused of writing like Hammett. But I never read anything by Hammett except when I was putting the *New Yorker* to bed. I worked on the *New Yorker* briefly. And I would have charge of going up there with him [Harold Ross], I could do it from my apartment, and they'd ring me over the phone, these, ah, guys that were doing the make-up. Or I could go up there, sometimes I went up with him into ... I think Greenwich was the place and I got a copy of *The Glass Key* and I would pick it up and try to read it, but I didn't really have my mind on it. It didn't prove a great deal as to whether it was any good or not any good. But by the end of four or five weeks I'd only read twenty pages of this book. I think to myself, "For Christ's sake, you can't like it too well." Those twenty pages are the only twenty pages of Hammett that I ever read. I have no famous recollection what *The Glass Key* was even about. And I met him one time, over at the Edward G. Robinson's. This somewhat wild-looking character with white hair he had, came charging up to shake my hand, and tell me how much he admired my writing and so on. Said he was Dash Hammett. And I wrung his hand, and I said what an honor it was, how glad I was to know him. And then I got away from this guy but quick, 'cause I had not read anything by him. Or at least this twenty pages didn't seem to be much to talk about. And that's all I know about Hammett. Chandler I've been accused of writin' like, too. I've never read one word of Chandler, except this *Orchid*. This old, this bald-headed old man raised his orchids, and had two nymphomaniac daughters—I think she's in some Chandler book. But was Kerry Wilson's account. That's all I know about Chandler. I met Chandler once. I used to run into him at parties: "Why hello, how've you been?" And he was married to a woman much older than he was, and we always heard that they were Hollywood's happiest couple. But it's coming out now in some biography of Chandler that in-between he got quite a little help outside. Got married to this elderly lady. She was rather attractive. But outside of that ... this one afternoon when Billy Wilder had me over to talk about this *Double*

Indemnity thing that he was working on at the time. I had no discussions with Chandler at all. I scarcely knew him.

McAleer: Who were some of your favorite writers?

JMC: My favorite book of all time I read when I was eight years old; I still read it every six months, I know it by heart but I keep reading it: *Alice in Wonderland.* I know this book, I know the titles of illustrations, I know every page of it, almost by heart and yet I keep reading it. Another favorite ... ? Casanova. I reread him every couple of years—his memoirs. I regard him as a very great writer and I think that if there had been no Casanova I doubt there would have been any Dumas, especially Dumas the elder. One book of Casanova deals with his visit to London, and in London Casanova fell for a girl so hard that he just was in agony about her and never caught her; she just played him for a sucker. She'd take a hundred pounds off him, and then say, "Well, maybe next time." And he just, he went nuts over this girl. But he also ... There was a woman there that he had rolled in the hay in Paris, or some place, and he reacquainted himself with her. And, apparently, she had worked out a peculiar racket. She would gain the acquaintance, somehow, of some noble lord, and then either fix him up with some girl that he wanted to lay, or in some other way entice him to a party. And then, using him as bait, get all kinds of other people to go to the party and various ones she'd try to lure money ... I thought to myself, "For God's sake, that's *Vanity Fair*!" And then it turns out that Thackeray, I read, some years ago, had admitted that this Casanova was the origin of Becky Sharp in *Vanity Fair*. And another reason I read Casanova, remember Casanova so well, remember then why he makes so much impression on me: when I was maybe eight years old there was a book around the house of my father's, who taught English at St. John's College before he became president of Washington College, had bought to give as a prize to one of his, in one of his English classes, it was a compendium of the great—I think it was called *Heroes of Song and Story*, something like the title of that. And there were all kinds of fantastically exciting episodes in it. One was called "Ox Arms." I didn't know what "Ox Arms" meant, but that was the title of it, at least as I ever read it, and, there was some people, adrift on a raft ... why it was called "Ox Arms" is gone from me. Then there was a story about the siege of Derry, renamed Londonderry, and now called Derry again. Oh, but one of these things, the best one in the book that I read, and reread and reread so many times I knew it by heart, was Casanova's *Escape From the Leads, in Venice,* and that was another reason that Casanova .... Later, when I saw the whole book, suddenly, I'm reading Casanova—ah, I knew this! By heart! And there it was exactly as I remembered it from this book. Oh ... ! Oh, in Baltimore, in my mother's home, I tried to find this book, I never was able to. It must have been given away or lost or something—but I, I didn't need it, of course, but I would like to have it as a title, to have an exact title of it, I'd never get it.

McAleer: Faulkner said that he felt the things worth writing about were the human heart in conflict with itself. What do you think of that idea?

JMC: It has no meaning for me. I don't know whether that's just one of those things that can mean anything or nothing. "The human heart in conflict with itself." How do you get in conflict with your own human heart? I don't understand that. To me, a story has to have some objectivity beyond subjectivity. That seems to be mainly a subjective theme, if I understand what he means. It has no meaning for me, actually, but I like a narrative to be concrete, not all inside some person. Of course a story, a good concrete narrative, has to be, it has to be about particular people. They have to have problems that we can understand and believe. But, even so, it seems to me that a good narrative moves objectively too. What else you got?

CHAPTER 3. THE ROXIE

"A lot of people write like James M. Cain. Few write as well."

—Robert B. Parker

"I didn't realize it at the time, but reading the books of James M. Cain and John D. MacDonald conditioned my writing eye and ear. They were training wheels. I discovered their work when I was still impressionable, read it and reread it - devoured it, really - long before it ever occurred to me to try writing myself."

—William G. Tapply

McAleer: You've been accused of writing like Hemingway. What do you say to that charge?

JMC: I was, had been, often enough accused of writing like Hemingway, and Hammet, and somebody else, I forget who, oh, Steinbeck ... but I was well on my way with my style, and six years older than Hemingway was, when his first short story that I ever read, called, "Fifty Grand" came out. And that story's not uninteresting. In a way, he and I did some copying of a certain kind. Oh, a woman; did you ever hear of Roxie Stimpson?

McAleer: No.

JMC: Well, Roxie Stimpson is the woman that had been married to Jess Smith. Jess Smith was the guy that Harry Dokerty went to in the Harding Administration. He was a bagman for the Harding Administration. He carried the money around, and, and collected the money. And he had one terrible fault: he couldn't keep his goddamn mouth shut. And Dokerty went to him, and put it up to him that as an act of loyalty to Harding, he owed it to Harding to kill himself. And, eventually, he did. [short pause] Maybe. Because maybe he killed himself, and maybe Dokerty put the pistol to his head and saved him the trouble. Nobody ever was sure. It was never proved on Dokerty, but it was suspected on Dokerty. But now, appears in Washington this woman, Roxie Stimpson, that she had been married to Jess Smith, the man who died. And, she went and told to the Senate Committee—what was that committee called—you'll think of it ... it's passed out of my mind, I get a little tired and I don't think of things. And she began to spill the truth about Dokerty and everything. She just talked. She meant to destroy Dokerty. By that time Harding was dead, but she meant to have her revenge against Harry Dokerty. These two couldn't get along, Jess Smith and Roxie, but in his agony of this proposition that Dokerty made, the only one he could turn to was her. And they couldn't live together as man and wife, they became so close in the light of this terrible situation that confronted Jess Smith, for Dokerty was plaguing him all over. Some time in there—here's where the "Fifty Grand" comes in, this paragraph in there that we all remember 'cause this is reprinted by Mack Sullivan in *Our Times*. They had an island about in the O'Hara River and a hunting lodge on it. And Jess Smith went there, and Roxie said, "and, at last," she said, "he could sleep—he knew what he had to do, and he could sleep," she said. "And then that Dokerty," she said, "came waking him up." You hated Dokerty for waking this poor bastard up, for something that he had to say. Now, in "Fifty Grand," the guy knows he's a fighter and he knows he can't win. He can't beat this other fighter known as the Bull Hog in this story, and finally he knows he's got to lose and when he admits to himself the truth, he can sleep. And then comes the manager, waking him up. Now, I give you one guess where Hemingway cut that idea, waking him up. Another thing in connection with that story is the sparing partner who tells the story. Uses the identical lingo that Roxie Stimpson used, and where her lingo affected me—and I think Hemingway too since he copied it in this story, you can't say he was indifferent to it—was this woman used every clammy cliché you ever heard of. She just talked like a Sinclair Lewis character. But in her mouth, these banal, cornball clichés somehow were reworked the way this Mexican girl reworks the songs she sings on the [Lawrence] Welk program: she does something to the words, just make them, you've never heard them before! And that's what this Stimpson woman did with these clichés and cornball expressions. She does something she did to them that gave them this terrible eloquence. Now you asked if something influenced my writing. She did to this extent: I never have any consciousness of copying, counting her directly, but, when in doubt as to whether some expressions I've put in this story is so head-on cornball, that I shouldn't use it, I will try to fudge it a little, give it a little fresh cadence or something, so I can say the inner, ah, essential ... . What's cornball, what's corny, may have great vitality. Save its vitality and give it a little rework the way she used to. By instinct she did it, of course I do it more consciously. I do a lot of rewrite, crossing out and tuning things up—that goes on all the time with me. Well it seems funny then: I have been accused of copycatting off Hemingway, getting back, I was well on my way, had a thoroughly developed style before I ever read this first thing I ever read by Hemingway, which was "Fifty Grand." I never had any consciousness of copying off him.

CHAPTER 4. PURE CAIN POLITICS

"James M. Cain was a master of less is more. Reading him is a pleasure; re-reading is sheer joy. "

—*Katherine Hall Page*

McAleer: Did you ever let politics or moralizing influence your writings as Hemingway did?

JMC: No. I started a story to be called "A Cocktail Waitress." I finished it as a matter of fact. And it doesn't satisfy me now and I'll be doing it over again. This was to be about a girl, a cocktail waitress, in a cocktail bar I invented to open out—down here in Northern Country Building, at the southern end of Hyatt's building. It's a county office building. And I had this saloon, this cocktail bar that was supposed to cater to this trade. And this girl, well, she got a job as a waitress in there. And that was all taken care of plausibly, and possibly. And, but then, little by little, she was to become a precinct captain and important in this tiny microscopic way, politically. And I covered this story very thoroughly. A lady that I know crossing the States drives me around, and she did drive me around. Over to Marlborough, covering the political background over there, and I got a lady in here that is a precinct captain. She gave me the dope on what a precinct captain does. And I got so loaded with this story—you wouldn't believe how much I knew, Christ Almighty, I had no more interest in it than, than if I had never done ... I just could not make myself get interested in it. And then told myself, "Well,

Cain, why don't you accept what you are. You're on the newspaper, you certainly have the brains, the skills, the journalistic know-how to be a political reporter." I could not make myself get interested in this field of journalism. Labor writing, labor reporter, I was interested in, as would still be interested in. I'm writing something along that line now for *Potomac Magazine* down here. I did four pages of it this morning before you came, but politics I cannot get interested in. I read a lot about it—who doesn't? But as for having any ideas about it, I have nothing that makes me search. Out of this story emerged an angle of this girl, and the story having nothing whatever to do with politics. But it turned out to be a pretty good lively story, and that, that was the thing that I finished and I made one mistake in: "Who were your lovers, pal?" I quoted Lawrence. I made a mistake on the story, thinking that my lovers were this woman and her little boy—little three-year-old boy—that figured as her motivation for her job in the cocktail bar that she had to pay for his board, with a sister-in-law that she had, after her husband—this woman's brother—got killed, and, it turned out I made a mistake. They were not the real lovers. The real lovers in the story were this man that came in—the very first day a man came in and she fell for him somewhat. And he for her, but .... I had her using him as a means to an end. Using him as a means of having a home for this child that she had. Where he was the big emotional fact in her life, and so the story has to be done over. It is half done over already. But then I interrupted it for something else.

As I mentioned I had no capacity to be interesting on that subject of politics. And I have some delay about this thing I'm writing now for *Potomac*. When they print it—I don't know, it's an argument against the crime of treason and advocacy of a pardon for this Japanese girl who applied for a pardon from Carter. And an argument that she ought to get it, but I'm writing a dissertation on treason. Something, I feel I know something about. Maybe I don't. And I have in here the great objection to treason that is so similar to heresy. And heresy is a crime that maybe they burned Joan of Arc for, but I don't really accept, and so. What else we got?

McAleer: Are you contending that treason is a negligible crime?

JMC: I think it's a crime that should be forgotten about. I don't think you'll ever succeed in repealing the Constitutional meaning of treason, but, you see, we couldn't accuse a traitor in connection with the Viet Nam War—you know why? Do you know why?

McAleer: No.

JMC: War was never declared. Treason to the United States now consists of levying war against them, or adhering to their enemies, giving them aid and comfort. Without a war we had no enemies. And congress never declared war. They gave Lyndon Johnson, on the basis of a wake in the water that may have been a shark and ma have been a torpedo fired from a boat that was never seen, a torpedo boat that was assumed to have an existence. On this fantastically slight casuistry, he was given authority to bombard the North Vietnamese. And on the basis of this congressional approval of a reprisal for this torpedo, the whole Vietnamese War was fought. That was the only legal basis it ever had. And yet this Dean Rusk would look us in the eye and talk about our commitment. We had no commitment of any kind to fight that war, and so, we could not have had the accusation of treason. Another thing about treason that bothers me is, say you blow up something here. They find out you're a British subject, you can't be accused of treason. But that guy who worked with you who is an American citizen, he can be accused of treason during a war. You both did the same thing and you can't be accused and he can be—I think that's wrong! I think that if you did all this down in Mexico, say, the Great War with Mexico, a grand jury on American soil can indict you for acts committed in Mexico City—I think that's wrong. I have the feeling that if an American citizen goes to Mexico and intrigues a broadcast against the United States, he should be told, "OK, if that's how you want it, you're now assumed Mexican allegiance ... but don't come back. You're a Mexican now." In other words, it costs a man his American citizenship to commit what otherwise would be an act of treason. But I don't think he should be prosecuted for it beyond that. On American soil, don't prosecute him for treason, or sedition, or whatever would come of it. But it's the same whoever does the act. About sedition, you can be a Chinese subject, and you could still be seditious against the United States. But to commit treason you must be an American citizen. Well, that simplifies it. I don't believe in forgiving it, but, if committed on American soil—but, I just don't like this treason thing. So I'm doing this article. Whether I sell it, I don't know.

McAleer: Concerning your fiction writing, what would you like to do in the future? What do you have plans for?

JMC: I'm going to finish "The Cocktail Waitress," and I never have plans for more than one draft. I don't know, books pop into your mind. I somewhat distrust these big process of writers that have trilogies, you know, great big plans. Christ Almighty, like Dreiser. He was writing *The Financier* and *Titan* and some other goddamn book. Jesus Christ, you couldn't, you couldn't finish these horrible books, they were just no goddamn good. Ah, he got a hold of a good one in this, *An American Tragedy* ... That's the one about the boy who drowned his sweetie-pie because she was going to have a child?

McAleer: Right.

JMC: Yes, and that was based on a real case and then he got executed for it. And that was, that was about something. I had something to do with that book. I was on the *New York World* when he was writing it and he wrote Mencken about it and Mencken wrote me: could I get Dreiser into the death house at Sing Sing? And I went down to [Barrack], the city editor, and told him about this, and he said I guess he could: "I could get him in if he'll do us an article on the basis of that representing *The World*, I think I could get him into the death house." So he agreed to do the article, and he got into the death house for this book. And he went. It was in the paper that he was going to Europe. And Barrack rang me up and said, "Where is my goddamn article?" But I said, "I don't know—haven't you got it?" And he said, "No!" and he said, "This guy is due to leave for Europe day after tomorrow or something and if I don't get that article, the court that I got a court order to get him into Sing Sing is going to feel that I was playing around, I was trifling with him." So I rang Mencken about it, and Mencken came down of Dreiser's head. Jesus Christ, if you don't think Henry Mencken can come down like a ton of bricks! And Dreiser came in pretty meek, saying that, he had to go to Europe, and that he had no time to do the article, and hows about an interview? And Barrack decided an interview would do it. But then he had the funniest attitude. Barrack says, "I guess we know next time Henry Mencken wants a favor what we do about it." He blamed all this on Mencken rather than on Dreiser. I don't know why he, in his [Barrack's] mind, blamed Mencken for it. And all this was *An American Tragedy*, getting ready for. That was a long time ago. This had to be over forty-five years ago. I little believed it could be that long, 'cause I wasn't old then. *The World* folded in 1931.

CHAPTER 5. CAIN ON CONTEMPORARIES

> "For me, it was always Cain's dialogue. The plots were marvels of construction, yes, but that dialogue—it was as stripped and calculating and icily-jazzed as his characters' black little hearts. Even now, very few writers come near his level in that regard."
>
> —*Dennis Lehane*

McAleer: Do you read contemporaries?

JMC: It seems to me I don't, but I guess I must. I don't read much fiction. I mostly specialize in reading background on the American Revolution. I have a book here with a dreadful title, *In Defense of Liberty* or some such Christ-awful title like that. But it's a very fine treatise on the background of the American Revolution. Quite a lot given over to King George the Third: the kind of man he was, how much he knew, what kind of life he lived, the way he was fixed up with this not very good-looking German wife—Caroline I think her name was—and the rest of it. It's all very interesting. Fresh stuff to me; maybe old hat to many people, but I don't think it's too old hat to everyone because I read an awful lot on this subject and most of it's fresh to me. A great deal about John Adams in there with stuff in it that I hadn't known. I mean he cuts from one to the other, there, the situation in England at the time George the

Third came to the throne. I read a lot in this field. What's the rest?

McAleer: You don't read many contemporary fiction writers?

JMC: Well, Vidal. I read his book on Burr, and Joyce [Carol] Oates. I generally manage to read something by her. It seems to me I read this thing on *Jaws*. And the *Exorcist*. I guess I read that. Was that a novel?

McAleer: Yes.

JMC: No, it was a picture.

McAleer: It was also a novel by William Blatty.

JMC: I guess .... I don't know if I read the novel. I saw the picture. There was a girl that used to come out here a lot. She became casting director on this *Exorcist* picture for all except the principals. And it had already been cast for the bit parts, and extras, and small walk-ons and so on. She cast them. Some people up the street—I don't drive a car anymore, and they had a car—and they took us over to the Mencken. [All of them were over there] and we had dinner over in the Baltimore, and when we came back, instead of coming here, the Dunkleys had us up there at their house. And she met these four very clean-cut nice-looking boys the Dunkleys had: 12, 14, 15 about that time. Now they're a little older. And when she became casting director of this picture—she'd been in show business (rather a good-looking girl) in her early thirties—she remembered these Dunkley kids and cast them, and put them in the picture. And they didn't know how to get into this place in Georgetown, where *The Exorcist* was shooting. And a girl across the street did know and offered to drive young Scott Dunkley in her car. And so she drove him in, and the director takes a look at it—he says, "I want that one, that there, I want that car!" So, suddenly, she was on the payroll of the picture with her automobile. They picked up the Dunkleys over five hundred dollars in payments on this connection that she had to have through this girl. And the girl across the street picked up a couple of hundred dollars. This was Thanksgiving Day, and they all got double pay for Thanksgiving. The car—'stead of rating fifty dollars a day, she got a hundred for it. Instead of getting thirty-seven dollars a day she got seventy-five or something like that.

McAleer: And you say you read *Jaws?*

JMC: *Jaws,* I read. This guy—that's a funny, interesting book—he just was a guy that didn't know how to write a novel. There's funny things in there. For example, he has a woman being bitten in half by a shark off the coast. And she ain't going to live very long when bitten in half by a shark. A great big shark, great white shark—they don't have him, but he put those great white shark, kind of *Moby Dick* effect in the book anyhow. Well, he knew all about what the woman thought about as she was dying, and her thoughts as she sees the shark fin approaching, and all the rest of it, off this place where she was taking a midnight swim—how'd you guess it? How he knew what she was thinking about, since she was lately deceased before he or anyone could talk to her was not ever explained. He just, what do you call it? ESP? Extrasensory Perception, apparently. And then all kind of stuff happened ’cause he knew all about out there in the middle of the ocean, how the guy thought about down in the cage before the shark bit him in two. Or how anyone knew what he was thinking about, I don’t know. Well, so he didn’t know how to write a novel—it was the biggest smash of any novel that had been written in my time, I guess. I have no recollection of any hit that big. Did you ever hear it? A tremendous smash hit. Another novelist: I’m laughing to myself over how this guy didn’t know how to write a novel (to an extent you don’t do much really laughing about it, but you think to yourself, oh, “if you had gone into English 43, they’d have explained to you about that!”) In spite of which, it’s a smash hit, and which is the only object the game ever had. What else you got?

CHAPTER 6. DIALOGING MARILYN MONROE AND THE TRIANGLE GIRLS

"If you want to read good dialogue you read James M. Cain. If you want to write good dialogue you read him twice. Then you wonder if you'll ever get it down as well as he did."

—Phil Lovesey

McAleer: What do you think of Faulkner?

JMC: I can't read Faulkner. Faulkner and Charles Dickens are two guys I can't read. I just simply can't read either one of them. I don't know what I object to in Faulkner. I don't accept for one thing his dialogue. I never knew any people that said "clumbed" for "climbed." "He clumbed." I never heard "clumbed." But his dialogue is all full of words like that. I cannot read him. And it's not only the dialogue. Clumsy dialoguing, if the rest of it interests you, you get accustomed to it. But, whatever it is he writes about — I cannot read him. I only read one thing by Faulkner in my life. That was a thing for the *American Mercury* he wrote called "I Think That Evening Sun Go Down." I think that was the title of it. I guess I read that and didn't like it at all. And after that I couldn't read anything by Faulkner. Yeah, what else?

McAleer: You don't think Fitzgerald was good at evoking character development through dialogue. Who do you think was good?

JMC: I'll tell you who's good: Arthur Miller, Sinclair Lewis. Arthur Miller was a genius at it. He was the one married to Marilyn Monroe. It came out in *Life*—I guess it was *Life*—there are certainly good looking girls aren't there. [laughter]—that he hadn't any right to write this play is not apparent to me. He had married her, they were divorced, he'd married again, he got on with his life. He could not have used the excuse that he had some stuff he had to emotionally get off his chest or something but he wrote this book—and I'm honest as the day is long—but the way he evoked this girl, his dialoguing in this play was beyond was beyond all belief *Life* said. She was very difficult to dialogue. Marilyn was what's called a triangle girl. They're girls that lived in that triangle between Hollywood Boulevard, Highland Avenue, Sunset. Makes a triangle. The Hollywood Bowl goes off one angle—Pepper Tree Lane they call it. It's off the Highland angle of this triangle. The Hollywood bowl Lane of maybe two to three hundred yards of trees and at the end of the Lane is the Hollywood Bowl that's off the triangle. But in this triangle a dozen apartment houses of one and two room apartments lived girls like Marilyn. They have one nice dress and one pretty good dress. They're known as party girls. A picture producer wants a girl or to have a night in the hay—he's giving a party—he tells the guy, "I've got something nice for you." And so he has a dinner at Perino's and this girl's there in her nice dress and she's introduced to this guy. Manners? pretty good. Appearance? very lady-like. Dress: fine. Maybe this producer bought it for her—he cuts himself a slice now and then. She regards this as part of how things are done. A girl I know that was one of them had some friend that I knew and she said she had a talking part. She has a bit part over at MGM. She said she was in the picture with young Doug Fairbanks and she said, "After the day's shooting you know what he did? He sent for her to come to his dressing room and they had a quickie right there in his dressing room." She says, "Wasn't that wonderful? He gave her fifty dollars," she said. I said to myself the kind of imagination that thinks that's wonderful—this was just a girl I ran into, you know at somebody's party. Now, Marilyn was that kind of girl—unquestionably. She was just a triangle girl and the days when she lived with Johnny Hyde of the Morris Agency that's all she ever aspired to be, but she was pretty spectacular looking just the same after she learned to comb her hair and dress and how to wear a tight skirt that she made her specialty, bulging her bottom into, and Arthur Miller caught this triangle. They had a way of talking. That peculiar lingo; it's different from anything I've ever heard. I've heard it a few times, after all, you live in Hollywood you meet some triangle girls at the party. Well, there was a big writer I knew—he wanted to borrow my apartment. I was living at the Hollywood Knickerbocker then. For three years I lived at the Knickerbocker. And well, he was a guy, I knew him quite well and very hard to tell him no, and I was going out so I thought—well, why not? So I said OK. So he came to dinner at the Knickerbocker bringing one of these girls and the other one he said, “The other one, your girl, will be along any minute.” I said, “I thought I made that clear? I’m not spending the evening with you.” Well, he had two girls, one for himself and one for me. He got his answers crossed up. He didn’t quite get straight that I wouldn’t be there or maybe he thought that when he had a good looking girl for me I’d be there anyhow. Anyway, this girl that he had, sat at dinner with us—I guess she ate dinner and she was quite well mannered ... to say well bred? I don’t know what it would mean. She went through the motions of being well bred, and was very friendly and nice and after I’d got home he was still in the apartment. The girls had gone and he had ordered some champagne up for them and, my God! This guy—the difference between how he had looked at dinner and how he looked now, completely ... not drunk out, but sexed out, was something to see. But his mouth was still dripping from the recollection of this evening—he was married to a big picture actress and I guess she didn’t have her mind on him. She had her mind on her next day’s work. She took herself very seriously [this girl he was married to]. A very celebrated actress. You’d know at once who she was. I don’t name any of these people—But the idea that when he got done with one he’d take a little rest and then board the other one. This was a terrific evening for him and I think psychologically he needed it, but what he needed was love in its pure physical, brutally, simple aspect without any overlay of much romance or anything else. But anyway, this girl I'm getting back to, Marilyn and the Arthur Miller dialoguing—I note her and I met plenty of others out there. Some of these girls were secretaries. Some of the secretaries you would have would be triangle girls and the secretaries would sort of tip off that if you wanted to work that evening she'd be willing. The idea being she'd pick up an extra fifty and you'd roll her a couple of times and then take her home and she'd give you a little kiss and she got out of the car and the next day be a secretary again. And that's how things were done out there. And I never got involved with anything like that myself, but the dialoguing on this play by Arthur Miller's to capture the way a triangle girls talks and thinks was beyond all praise—it was just simply terrific. So you ask me who I think dialogued well—I'm telling you there's an instance. Now, Sinclair Lewis, how he dialogued, he dialogued the kind of people maybe I could dialogue too pretty well. I wouldn't do too bad, but they weren't people that would be presenting too many difficulties. Some of them did—some of the dialogue in *Elmer Gantry*—the three preachers sitting around, sort of reviewing their lives that night as to whether they would do it this way if they had their lives to live over again. That's very beautiful dialogue. The subtlety and exactitude of that scene with the preachers is just terrific. In addition to Lewis and Miller, I'll tell you who else dialogues well is this girl Oates. She's a very distinguished writer and another who dialogues well is Gore Vidal, and he's very distinguished. The Oates girl though, I take some exception to her ... the bones of her story, the essence of it. Sometimes it seems to me she's very disregardful of the easy ... well, they don't have to be easy credibilities, but it has to be credible. Sometimes only the fantastic in certain circumstances—the utterly incredible you say would be the credible. Like the rabbit hole in *Alice in Wonderland.* But in some of her stories it just seems she makes it easy for herself by saying it happened without explaining how it happened. You say to yourself, "Well, for Christ's sake, why didn't you sit down and work on that and get it right." And so, OK, I'm willing to believe that the guy was put into a truck or something and rode off somewhere and that murder was never proved. There was some book that involved that in hers. It came out about two or three years ago. She gets 'em out you know every month and a half. But in general she has vitality. Her stories do something to ya. So she's very good. Well, that's all I can think of now. What else you got there?

CHAPTER 7. THE LOVE REC

> "The term 'thriller' gives expectations few books live up to. Perhaps ten or fifteen genuine examples have ever been written, and Cain is the author of two of them. *Double Indemnity* and *The Postman Always Rings Twice* are taut, tense, exquisitely plotted stories that involved and excited me from the first page to the last."
>
> —*Peter Lovesey*

McAleer: How did you get your start in writing?

JMC: Start writing? I don't know any answer to that question. I have been writing since I was twenty-two years old. Trying to write. Some of it, in the beginning, was some short stories off to the magazines and get 'em back. Then I went in the newspaper business. Of course, you wrote a story at ten o'clock at night and then two hours later its in the paper. Then an effort at plays in New York. Editorial writing in New York. Newspaper business in a little more definite way. Then, a play I wrote in New York. And it was produced out on the road and then brought in and—not ever brought in on Broadway. Then, California and at picture writing. Not very enthusiastic on my part. I wanted the money, but I really didn't like pictures. But then, after two ... three starts at novel-writing, I wrote a novel based vaguely, not directly, but—brought into my mind by the Jed Grey Case. You may not remember that celebrated murder case. Now, I met a man, had met a man in New York. Continued our friendship in Hollywood. And he had a great effect on my writing. Until then, I didn't know what story I was trying to tell. But after I'd been seeing a great deal of him, I began to realize that his insistence on love story applied to me. He had a great affect on Hollywood. His name is Vincent Lawrence. I mention this man in my Preface to *Three of a Kind*, and told the story in there of my relationship with him. And, his effect on Hollywood was this: When he went out there, they had what you might call the Mix-Master system of love story. They's have the guy see the girl through their flower shop window. And then, by some arrangement, he'd take her to the amusement park, and they'd go through Shoot the Chutes, and Gravity Railroad, and Cyclone, and God knows what. And at the end of this "montage" as they called it, they were supposed to be in love. He wouldn't have it. He said it's just too easy and it's no goddamn good.

McAleer: I will. I'll make sure.

JMC: He [Lawrence] said you have to have what he called a "love rec." I have no idea how that "wrack" is spelled. Whether it's w-r-a-c-k, r-a-c-k, or where the word, "wrack" applies.[2] I never found out and every time I tried to get it out of him, he'd get sore as if I must be pretty dumb even to ask, and that's all I can tell you. But that's what he called it. What he meant was ... a verse of

---

[2] Cain biographer Roy Hoopes spells it "rack." For reasons explained in the footnote on page 45, this edition uses "rec." —*Ed.*

poetry. And he would illustrate what he meant by a moving picture. *Susan Lenox* was the name of the picture, with Garbo in it and Gable. And in this picture, Garbo was a farm girl who got fed up on how she was treated out on the farm. And she threw the whip down over a pair of horses and went galloping off by herself and winds up tired, and hungry, and depressed—at a house she turns in at. Where, by funny coincidence, Gable was living, all alone. He's a surveyor laying out the grades for a new railroad they're gonna build. And he asks her in and stables her horses for her. Telephones her people to come and get 'em, or something like that to take care of the horses. Got them out of the way. Puts her up for the night, and, like a gentleman, doesn't try to do anything to her. And, next day, they decide to go fishing. And she catches a fish. It was this moment that Lawrence always would come back to illustrate what he meant. She catches this live thing—they do things that way in pictures—wriggling on its hook, a good big fish. She grabbed him and said, "I'll cook him tonight for your supper!" And then realized she betrayed herself. And he'd realized it too. And he folded her into his arms. And that, that moment of poetry, inadvertent, a moment a moment that catches him by surprise—he insisted the picture had to have.[3] And he'd get a job in pictures, and they'd have this story conference. And

[3] This is the moment that the love is recognized; thus, "love rec."—*Ed.*

they'd wait while he gave the verdict. While they waited, he'd always play a baseball game. Each take a minute as pitcher, taking a signal from the catcher, throwing the catcher-man off first base, raising his club up for the return throw, throwing the guy—and they'd all watch this baseball game going on. And pretty soon: "You got no lovers, pal." This dreadful verdict would come out: "You got not lovers." Meaning: you don't have a moment of poetry, there's nothing here to make a story out of. So, OK, we take it from there.

McAleer: OK.

JMC: Wait a minute, I ain't done yet. You want me to tell how this thing started?

McAleer: OK, go ahead.

JMC: So getting back to this murder story that I had some idea. I got closed out of a studio, Columbia. The last day Harry Kolm, the president of the studio, told his ace writer, ah—Bob Riskin was his name, married to a girl named Fay Wray—sent him off to talk to me, and find out what made me tick. What he wanted to find out really was whether I ticked. 'Cause I bothered Harry Kolm—he couldn't figure me out. And Bob Riskin, when he got through, he said, "You have the strangest mind." He said, "You seem to think that every story is some kind of algebraic equation. That if you transform it and transform it and transform it, you can come up with the perfect story." He said, "it's not like that. It has to be your story you're trying to tell." So I go home and this novel that I'd been vaguely thinking of writing kept coming back. And: OK, it'll be my story: a couple who knocked the girl's husband off, and this murder is that big love rec—that's the moment of poetry. But I said to Lawrence "Why can't the whole thing be a love rec? Why does it just have to be one moment? Well, this was an idea he couldn't get used to. And he never did accept my opening shot between the guy and the girl in that story. Anyway, I write it. And in that novel, incidentally, there is a beginning of this style that I have got to be so well known for. I kept telling myself on that final rewrite, "Fast means fast—tell it, get on with it." And I would condense three, four chapters into just a few lines of dialogue at the opening of the next chapter and get on with it. And the name of the story at the time was *Bar-B-Q*. Which you see out on every sign in California. But I retitled it on the basis of the conversation with Lawrence I had one time [and called it] *The Postman Always Rings Twice*. This was this ... I was utterly frightened when I got through with this thing, as a result of all this condensation. It was only one hundred and fifty-nine pages long. And it was declined by the publisher. He turned it down; just no good at all. A very snooty letter I get from him. But I sent Walter Lippman a copy of this story. And my wife insisted—she said, "You promised Louder"—as she called him, she had a thick, Finnish accent—"that you would send him a copy. And you have an extra copy." So I sent him a copy. And two hours after the publisher's letter came, I get this wire from Lippman: "Think *Bar-B-Q* sure fire. Want authority to deal with Macmillan. And he got this authority so quick you couldn't see "Go."—my wire return. And Macmillan didn't want it. Then he went over to Knopf, and managed to stuff it down—that's the first publisher—his throat, anyway. And this story, my publisher accepted very unwillingly, and disbelievingly. He had no confidence in this story. And a fellow that reviewed books for the American News Company, I think was the name of it. He stretched out the story in about two lines: "Guy and a girl knock off her husband for the money and so on. If this one doesn't smash I'm going to look for another job." And suddenly I was famous all over the country with this story. It was a big hit. And that's how I came to write novels. Answering your question. Now, then, you had something to say?

McAleer: Right. How did you arrive at the title, *The Postman Always Rings Twice?*

JMC: That's all in the Preface to *Three of a Kind.* I was in looking through the Château Élysée—Lawrence had an apartment. Well, we lived downtown, but he kept this apartment on the Shadow-Flysees. Big swank apartment house, not far from where I lived. And he got a telegraph about his first play. He mailed it to a producer in New York. Then he said, "I'd keep watching for the mailman to come with his answer." And then he said, "Ah, to hell with this, you go nuts watching for the mailman." Then he said, "So then I'd go upstairs, but then," he said, "I caught myself waiting for his ring." He said, "No fooling around about that ring, either. He always rang twice."

And he went on to tell me. But I interrupted and I said, "Hey, wait a minute, Lawrence. I think you're giving me a title for that story that I had been calling *Bar-B-Q*." I said, "*The Postman Always Rings Twice*." "Hey, hey, hey," he said. "I kind of like that," he said, "and it sure rang twice for Chambers, didn't it?" And I said, "That's the idea. OK," I said, "Then that's it." The publisher thought it was a dreadful title. He hated it, but he had to take it. Well, the title was so bad that they even wrote Broadway songs about it: "The postman always rings twice, the iceman walks right in," and things like that. And so the book did very well. That's my story of my first book and the story of the title. The Preface of *Three of a Kind* is the story of that title. OK, what else?

McAleer: Did you feel when you were writing *The Postman Always Rings Twice* that you wanted readers to be sympathetic towards the narrator? Did you have that in mind at all?

JMC: I have no recollection of having any feeling about it. I just let him tell the story. He's about to die, you know. At that time, I didn't use tape recorders as I do now. I have the character type up his story. That's a new development. It started somewhat for me by Billy Wilder, when he had the idea during *Double Indemnity,* by having Fred MacMurray using a tape recorder and telling the story, and then cutting to what he's telling about. But I let him tell a story and I figured that if what he's telling is interesting enough, the reader will stay with it without worrying too much about whether he's for him or against him, or anything about it. In the end he finds out that one reason this man is being so candid is he feels he may have to die. He's not sure yet, he's waiting for a stay of execution. But he doesn't get it. And in the final chapter, he realizes ... . The last words of the book are "No stay" or something like that. That's all the answer I can give you on that one.

Chapter 8. So That Was My Trouble in Hollywood

"Cain made it seem easy, but only if you've tried it yourself do you realize how difficult it is to master the genre as skillfully as he did."

—Edward D. Hoch

McAleer: Do you agree with the critics who contend that Hollywood devours writers.

JMC: What the hell does that mean? Devours them to this extent. When you're writing for pictures you can't do anything else. You can't, on the weekends, do your own novel. It just won't work that way. To that extent—and there are writers who could do their own writing and, get so enamoured of the picture payroll. I'll give you a writer for example, that sat out there. Aldous Huxley, a very brilliant English writer. I didn't know him well, but he was to dinner one night. And he seemed to know who I was and treated me very respectfully, and I certainly treated him with respect. But he sat around for five months out there, waiting for the chance to talk to Hump Stromberg—he's a producer, for Christ's sake! Hump Stromberg keeps Aldous Huxley sitting around in a room for five months. I don't know. I'll tell you a conversation I had with a girl. She didn't aspire to eat at the lunch table where I ate at. Where I and where distinguished people like me had lunch. Christ knows—some of them were distinguished and some of them were well-paid. Anyway, she had to eat lunch somewhere else, at another table. But she would generally be waiting for me at the junction of the walk from the studio commissary metro over to the walk that—junction of that walk and the one that led to the Iron Lung, as it was known as. The Thalberg Building where we had all our offices, and she had her office, and I had mine. And she'd walk over to the Iron Lung with me. And one day she seemed lower or down. I said, "Well, what's the matter? Somebody poured gravy on your ice cream, doll?" She said, "The usual: My option. It's coming up. And I guess they're going to take it out." And they will. I just don't know. In Hollywood, you're on a seven-year contract. But there were six month options. They'd take up the option for six months, and then at the end of that, the question was whether they were going to exercise their option for the next six months, when you go a hundred-dollar raise—maybe. And so I said, "Well, listen to who's bragging." I said, "Options, for Christ's sake." I said, "Yeah, I ain't got no options on me." I said, "I'm on a day to day basis." I said, "We could even say hour to hour. We could say minute to minute!" I said, "Anytime now the foreman could walk into my office, turn the light out over my typewriter, and that would be it." "Ah, for Christ's sake," she said, "will you shut up? And let someone who really has a problem talk." "Well, OK," I said, "Gee ... ." The she said, "You're, you're, you're same old lecture, everybody knows it. And so, fat chance you would be fired. I wish you'd shut up. I've got real trouble." I said, "Can I have that over again? What did you say?" "Oh," she said, "it's the thing now. Everybody, they all got one. Hunt Stromberg has Aldous Huxley. Arthur Freed has Bob Nathan. And Arthur Hornblow has you. So," she said, "fat chance you would be fired. Shut up! And let somebody talk that has real trouble." Oh! This was a funny idea to me. I never heard of anything like it. There was an element of truth in it, I think. I can't say—because Arthur kept me working on this story long after I should have been closed out. I think to have a distinguished dinner guest when he'd be giving a dinner. And, someone that knew one of his lines from another. And, well, to that extent, Hollywood could devour writers. I suppose Huxley was being devoured in a way by Hunt Stromberg. Then—well, actually, I think Huxley wrote some book about a picture producer, if I'm not mistaken. And, what's the name of the Irishman that lived up with Sheila Grant? *The Great Gatsby*, who wrote it?

McAleer: Fitzgerald.

JMC: Scott Fitzgerald. Yeah, Scott Fitzgerald. When he actually wrote some pictures and one or two of them were produced—I suppose pictures devoured him in a way. He wrote a book finally called *The Last Tycoon*. I think that was the title of it. More notes for a story—I never heard of writing about writing a novel that way. I should lecture Scott Fitzgerald on how to write a novel. But it seemed to me to be a somewhat stumblebum half-hearted-go-through-the-motions way of kidding yourself you were writing a novel. I have it upstairs someplace. This, *Last Tycoon.* I've actually read it. It's just no goddamn good. It's supposed to be about, Irving Thalberg, who Fitzgerald professed admiration for. I don't know how or why. Thalberg was the coldest, most unlikable son of a bitch! A great genius at pictures, but as a human being! I talked to him once: and he came and summoned all us writers in one of the projection rooms—projection room is kind of a theater—and told us that if anybody was joining this new writers' union they was having, then we could just look for another job, or something. And he was very cold, it struck me. He had a funny way of pursing his mouth up in an odd kind of way, as though he didn't then have enough blood in his body. I think that was part of his trouble. He was married to a girl, named Norma Shearer. And she was known as the First Lady of Hollywood. And she had a tremendous success as a picture actress. And after he died, she went out like a light. They went in together parts. But it turned out her acting—she was kind of a Trilby to his Svengali.. That all her scenes he'd rehearse with her the night before she'd go on the set. She'd do them for him, and he'd direct her, and take charge of her, and tell her how to do it. And then she'd go on the set the next day and do it the way he had said. And made a great actress out of her. But after he'd died, there was no one to give her that special direction that he furnished her. And she just went out like a light. I don't think she did three pictures after he died. Well, you'd better check on that. I don't guarantee, but that's what I heard. But

I'm not a very good commentator on Hollywood and pictures. I don't really know to much about them. I do and I don't. I was out there. I was with picture-people all the time. I worked with the studios years on end. And yet I was never of the business. I had one reason that excluded, one thing excluded me: I just didn't like pictures. Didn't and don't. I never look at them on TV. And since I came East, I've seen five pictures. My wife and I went to see the picture about—*Kon-Tiki*, the big shark trailed along in back of the boat. And *High Noon* we saw. And *Little Shiva*, we saw. And after she died, the people next door took me to see—they knew my interest in the big cats and they took me to *Born Free*, and as a kind of thing to get my mind of my bereavement. And I took them to see *Virginia Woolf.*

McAleer: What about *The Exorcist*?

JMC: That one I think I read. And those five pictures are all I've seen here in the twenty some years I've lived her. So that was my trouble in Hollywood.

CHAPTER 9. *GATSBY* AND I HATE FREAKS

> "James M. Cain's novels were my introduction to noir fiction. There have been many writers since with a flair for the Dark Side of human nature, but none with the same deft touch."
>
> —*Sue Grafton*

McAleer: You said earlier that you didn't think Fitzgerald went through a good procedure in writing a novel. Why is that?

JMC: I don't think it was his regular procedure. I think ordinarily when he started to write a novel he wrote it, he just didn't stick down a set of disconnected paragraphs—really notes. I suppose I make notes for a novel. My notes are an outline, an outline, an outline. I write twenty outlines before I get done with it. Boy I get this outline down to about two to three pages of handwritten script. Then I'm done with it. I mean I've boiled it and boiled it and boiled it 'til I know it by heart. And then I do character sketches of my characters. You'd be surprised how just simply toying around with a character it becomes real to you and yet you don't, you don't do much inventing of far-fetched peculiar characteristics. You just—you don't know where the character came from, but you play around with her and pretty soon she seems real to you. And then a chapter outline I do. I suppose I do all those things, but I would certainly never let it be published. Maybe he didn't intend it to be published. Maybe Sheila Grant or somebody published it after he died without his knowing they were gonna do it. He works his way, but I don't think—I have some reason for thinking that's not the usual way he worked. I think it was a man near the end of the line and more or less knew he was at the end of the line that was trying to pick himself up to go through the motions again. That would be my diagnosis of him. So Fitzgerald has certain limitations that were very peculiar. He had very little capacity to evoke character through dialogue. In *Gatsby*, I never heard anybody in my whole life call people "Old Sport." It just didn't ring true to me. I didn't accept it. And if you read the dialoguing in *Gatsby*—which is his best book, or is the only book that I was able to read of his, it's not a good book except the last fifty pages of it. This afternoon, where these five or six people out there on Long Island get bored with themselves on Sunday and drive into New York and take a suite at The Plaza—I guess they take it to pass the time of a Sunday afternoon and get drunk—suddenly the book comes to life—it lives and from there on to the end I would say the story gets a little too good with the death of Gatsby. Very effective where this Gatsby car hits a guy's wife and without stopping goes on and leaves her dead on the road and the guy in a rage notes whose car it is and goes and kills Gatsby not knowing that who was driving the car wasn't Gatsby, but this woman he was stuck of. She drove the car this same Sunday afternoon then on the way back she hit the woman and she very much in character went on without stopping and so he goes and kills Gatsby in reprisal for what he thinks Gatsby did, not knowing that the woman did it. The woman never did anything to exculpate Gatsby or save his life or anything at all. That lived. I would say this killing of Gatsby—it struck me as a little too good, but when a story's rowing up to that point he has to increase the voltage and so I even accept that fifty pages of it,, but the rest of the book—I just never believed, I never believed he was a bootlegger. I never believed that Fitzgerald knew a goddamn thing about bootlegging or had taken the trouble to find out anything about bootlegging. You took it on faith that Gatsby was a big bootlegger. I didn't take it on faith. The whole picture of this mansion that he had down there, which I heard later was Herbert Swope's house that Fitzgerald knew very well. I knew Swope very well, but I was never at his house. He called himself "Executive Editor" of The World. Anyone else would have said "Managing Editor" but Swope had to be executive editor. Until that Sunday afternoon, Gatsby had become utterly incredible to me. The parties he was supposed to be throwing, well Christ, you seen one keg of gin you've seen 'em all. So—what else?

McAleer: You talked about credibility and the fact that Fitzgerald, you felt, never knew a bootlegger. Are your own stories drawn from your own experiences?

JMC: I don't know how to answer that. One time a producer in Hollywood, a big producer named (Kelly?) Wilson, he died, but he was very big. He produced this

Andy Hardy series—you know that of course this judge and so on played by Mickey Rooney—and he had this big booming voice that MGM used on a whole lot of sound tracks like the Iwo Jima thing. He did the sound track on that documentary. And one time, talking to me he said, "I hate freaks!" I said, "What do you mean, freaks?" He said, "By freaks I mean characters so far-fetched and peculiar that I just don't believe it." I guess he was talking about a character in Chandler. "OK," he said, "So he's an old bald headed guy. Well, we all know an old bald headed guy." He said, "Who raises orchids. Wait a minute," he said, "I don't know an old bald headed guy that raises orchids. Well, could be. How do you raise them? I'd like to know more about it. You gotta have a hothouse, don't ya? Pretty expensive. A lot of trouble. Well, so OK he raises orchids—who has two nymphomaniac daughters. You take this son of a bitch and drop him in the lake. I don't believe him. He just made him up. He's a freak. That's what I mean by freak. He was just a farce. Then he said, "That's why I like your books. They're about dumb people, that I know. That I meet every day. There's nothing far fetched or freakish about 'em." He said, "You put them in interesting situations. That's why I like your books," he said. So this question is something about real life. For example, take a book of mine that was about something somewhat off beat, *The Moth* which was about a young, ex-football player and singer who I put through the depression of the early 1930s. Well, I came to that book honest. I was living in Burbank briefly at the time and

I'd drive out past the Warner Brother's Studio and be held up to enter the Town of Burbank. A freight train parked on the side there. This would happen quite a few times. The freight would seem to arrive right about the same time. Maybe I'd been in Hollywood to some picture show or something. This would be my 11:15 every night and silhouetted against the dark of Burbank itself would be these heads on the top of these freight cars. Not just two or three of them, or three or four dozen—three or four hundred of 'em! And it seemed so terrible a thing that these boys—most of them just boys—couldn't stay home anymore. Had no place to go but the top of this horrible freight car and I knew because I'd covered a story called, "Dead Man" that involved me with a freight train that I'd covered downtown. I knew that they were all gonna be put off this freight train three or four miles up the line when the engineer would slow down as they went past a certain field and the brakemen would come back, say, "Rise and shine boys. Get off! Get off!" And he'd just brush 'em off like caterpillars off a twig. I used that expression in the story. Well, I took it from there, but I did it honest, I think. I went downtown to one of the missions on Los Angeles Street and found a guy—apparently intelligent guy named, Moran and I'd pick him up every day and ride around with him. I kicked him with a couple of suits, an overcoat, nice pair of shoes that I had—they all fit. He was about my size and suddenly from looking fairly raggedy-tack, he was nicely dressed in these suits that I kicked him with. And he'd ride around with me and tell me stories—he was a hobo—what life on the road was like. And he kept on talking about a 'jungle.' And I knew that there was something about this 'jungle' I don't understand. I'd read about jungles in Jim Tully and Jack London. They all had something about the 'jungle'. But he knew where there was a jungle and we rode out there. Sittin' around there, a terrible thing to see, was an old hobo—I say old—a hobo in his sixties ain't young believe me he's an old man. And this guy didn't look like a hobo really. He looked like some ex-bookkeeper or something. But there he was at the end of the plank. But then I found out what a jungle is. Do you know what a jungle is?

McAleer: I don't.

JMC: It's a water pipe. With a spigot on top. Straight out of the ground alongside the railroad tracks. Here and there they need water for this and that and they have these spigots. And that's a jungle. And the thought crossed my mind: in Annapolis, our house was maybe fifty to a hundred yards from Humphrey's Hall where the college dining room was. And when the dining room would close—any dining room attracts rats, I don't care how good the dining car steward has the work done, there's gonna be enough food dropped around and so on that rats can make a living on it. Well, these rats of course would come trooping down to our house and my father would put arsenic for them around, on cheese, I guess that's how it was done, but he'd go around cutting off all water, in the house. He said, "If there's any water in the house, God, any running water in the house, God help ya, they'll get up in the walls and die there and then," he said, "you got a thing on your hands." He cut off all water, and made sure there was no running water of any kind in the house. He said, "When they eat the arsenic then they'll go out running outside for water to drink because it causes a dreadful thirst." And so, I kept thinking about these rats and the water that they had to have, and that's what a jungle is. Well, that may have been in this book, *The Moth,* I called it. So with Moran's help I covered this story. It was not personal experience and yet, by the time I got done with him I knew plenty about the life that a hobo lives. I knew plenty about it. So to that extent the book was first hand, yet of course, it wasn't. The first novel of mine, *The Postman Always Rings Twice,* was about a roadside sandwich joint and a filling station they had along the side and some shacks outside that they rented for cabins, and by that time, I had done some background work on restaurants. I had done some in connection with some writing I did for Collier's. I ghosted some stuff for a girl, "A Child's Waitress," and I had to go into restaurants and so on and but I used a lot of that background, that left over background for *Mildred Pierce*. But I had no occasion to do much about the restaurant business in *The Postman Always Rings Twice*. I probably did have in the chapters that I knocked out. But when I got done with it there was very little about the restaurant business and plenty about what was done upstairs. That, it turned out, is what they wanted to read about rather than hot dogs. And so, in a sense there's first hand knowledge, but not exactly out of my life. I never wrote, I had a little, for example, this last book that I have called, *The Institute*.

Chapter 10. Packed and Loaded: John McAleer and James M. Cain Interview August 23, 1976

> "I think Cain's a hell of a good storyteller, a marvelous storyteller. That way of telling a story—I don't think you can do it any better than *The Postman Always Rings Twice*. It can't be done better than that. I think it's a perfect job. If I were asked to name the living writer who I think has stuck most closely to that idea—stick to the story, stick to the goddamn story—it probably would be James M. Cain. There's not a word in Cain that does not apply to the story he's telling you."
>
> —*Rex Stout*

John McAleer: What's your opinion of Edmund Wilson?

James M. Cain: Edmund Wilson wrote two main pieces about me, one "Boys in the Backroom," where he put me at the top of his list at that time, but somewhat patronizingly, and the other, a review of *Past All Dishonor,* in which he said I'd done my research in projection rooms, though how he knew, as he probably was never in a projection room, or Virginia City, which I was writing about, or a mine, the theme of my book, though I'm a miner and a member of the United States Mineworkers of America—this I don't know. But Joseph E. Jackson, of the *San Francisco Chronicle* (I think), the only reviewer who actually knew much about Virginia City, at the time of my novel, praised it extravagantly, particularly the mining background. So you pays your money and you takes your choice. Wilson, in spite of the vast erudition, was prolix to the point of tedium, and often, in plain English, a 100,000-word pain in the neck.

McAleer: How do you rank Joyce Carol Oates?

Cain: Joyce Carol Oates wrote a nice piece about me for Madden (I think it was he who got out an anthology of pieces)[4], and I greatly admire her own work, though it is often utterly irrational and disregardful of the simple probabilities. Yet, I don't think she really likes me, which doesn't stop my liking her, particularly that incredibly delicate, slender, utterly graceful neck.

McAleer: Do you pay much attention to critics?

Cain: I have no choice of critics and what they say of my work, and in fact don't think much about them. Hemingway, I thought, made a dreadful blooper when he let what was said about him in *Death in the Afternoon*, color the rest of his work, so he kept putting the word "obscenity" into his dialogue, and in various way betraying that he wasn't writing a novel, but a reply to his various critics. But what did he expect? He actually did in that book, have the Old Lady from Dubuque

---

[4] *Tough Guy Writers of the Thirties*, ed. by David Madden. Carbondale, Illinois: Southern Illinois University Press, 1979.

saying: "So we are both talking horse shit." I never knew an old lady from Dubuque to talk that way, and if they said he was the boy with the piece of chalk, he could have said to himself perhaps that one time they were right, and got on with his life. Instead of which he let it be a monomania with him. They don't ride me that hard—I mean I don't let them ride me that hard. And I tell myself, as for example in regard to this dreadful piece about *The Institute* in the New York Times Book Review, he could be right, think it over.

McAleer: Do you know of any compendium of your writings?

Cain: Some years ago a checklist was published of my "works," but I forget by whom and when. I have a certain obtuseness in these matters.

McAleer: What makes someone a writer? Is it something they are born with?

Cain: Who knows what moves one to be a writer? I was sitting in Lafayette Park, Washington, one day, meditating on my misspent life (at the age of 22) and the collapse of my effort to become a singer, when out of the blue it came to me, "I'm going to be a writer." But actually, if anyone in my family had bothered to read the signs, I was headed for being a writer since I was eight years old. For example, my father smoked Turkish Trophy cigarettes, and for 70 of these coupons you could get a fountain pen. I, of course, fell heir to the coupons, and all I ever ordered, one after the other, was a series of fountain pens. An omen, but no one paid any attention. You can't decide to be a writer—you can decide to try a book, but not to be anything. You will be what God made you to be, without your having much to do with it.

McAleer: Are your stories ever based on your personal experiences?

Cain: I've never consciously written, in fiction, from personal experience.

McAleer: Are any of your stories or characters based on people or situations you've encountered?

Cain: I've never based a story, consciously, on people I know.

McAleer: Do you write more than one draft when writing a book?

Cain: I rewrite so much I lose track of how many drafts it takes to finish a book. At least four or five, sometimes more. I've cut down the number in recent years by outlining, not only of story, but of characters, etc., before I start the text. This sidesteps a lot of false starts I used to make.

McAleer: How long does it generally take you to complete a final manuscript?

Cain: I wrote one story in 15 days *(The Embezzler)*, with the IRS after me for $3,000.00 due on a previous book. *Mildred Pierce* took me a year and *Mignon* probably ten, altogether. Yet *The Embezzler* is a better book. If it takes you too long, you could be suspicious of the idea. It ought to take work and plenty of it, but too much work is not a good sign with a book.

McAleer: Would you consider yourself a good judge a human nature? Must a writer be so?

Cain: This question reminds me of Somerset Maugham's remark, in *The Summing Up,* that though a knowledge of human nature was no doubt a prerequisite for a novelist, he knew no way around studying it. I've had my characters praised, and do, as I've said, sketch them out, mainly for background, names (very important, very difficult, to get exactly the right name, one you're comfortable with, one that matches the character), and yet I have little capacity to analyze them, or go into their base characteristics. The same is true of my capacity, or lack of it, to penetrate people in real life. I've often said, of Sara Mencken, the girl Henry married in middle age, that she had a costly gift, the capacity to "see through" people—it cost him most of his friends before they got done with it. But I don't have it. I have little capacity to analyze my characters—I outline how big they are, how old they are, how they dress, how they talk, etc.—but their inner works I know little about consciously. I must, intuitively, know them a bit, but not consciously.

McAleer: As a writer do you set goals for yourself?

Cain: At the start of my career, I laid out no program for myself, except to try and find out how the trick was done. I had no success at all until I met a man named Vincent Lawrence, to whom my *Postman* is dedicated—he lent me the money to eat on while I was writing it, and in all ways took an interest. He was a narrative theoretician beyond all belief in his encyclopedic profundity, and had as much effect on Hollywood, as I've written in various places, as he had on me. He clarified my ideas for me, and all of a sudden, from having made a mess of various efforts to write novels, I leveled off with one that finally came off—my first published novel, *The Postman Always Rings Twice,* originally called *Bar-B-Q.* His ideas applied more to plays and screenplays, less directly to novels, but I didn't know that then (he talked Love Story, morning, noon, and night, which is what a playwright worries about, where a novelist is really more concerned with career, a character's relation to his destiny—but my novels are really plays transformed into a narrative so his ideas were perfect for me.) So he was a tremendous influence on me, and clarified what I was trying to do. He was also an influence on Hollywood, where they had a very naïve idea of love story, and perfunctory approaches to it. He made them take it seriously, and try to get quality into it.

McAleer: Do you have a favorite book or author?

Cain: My favorite book at the age of 8, and my favorite book now, is *Alice in Wonderland.* I must know it by heart, but I reread it every six months anyhow. I think its rhythmic quality, especially the poetry, is part of its appeal to me, as it is with W. S. Gilbert, whom I also know by heart, whole pages of him. The only writer I consistently can't stand is Charles Dickens. Somehow, those names, like *Chuzzlewit*, put me off, and the whole man is so dreadfully head-on and obvious that I do throw up on the carpet when I think of him. [Compiler's note: Rex Stout said that he would rather have written *Alice in Wonderland* than any other book in English written in the 19th century.]

McAleer: What is your writing schedule?

Cain: I write every day, after intending not to, to take a day off and relax. The, promptly at 11:30 I go to work, and work about four hours—or until I tire. Sometimes, I'm done in an hour especially if the work goes well and I have two or three highs, spots where it really excites me. Highs are very exhausting, and if I quit at the end of an hour, it's really a good sign.

McAleer: What book do you think is your best work?

Cain: My best book is the one which sold the most copies, so far as I'm concerned, and by that test, my *Postman* leads the list, with so many editions I've completely lost track[5]. I'm quite vain of the fact that it's still in print, and still making me a living.

---

[5] *Postman* sold 1,843 new copies in 2009, according to Nielsen BookScan. –*Ed.*

McAleer: Do you handle more that one project at a time?

Cain: I always have a plan for one book ahead. Beyond that, I let the idea come when I'm ready to do something about it.

McAleer: Do you ever wish you could rewrite or make any changes to your works?

Cain: You ask a question I've never asked myself, so there's no point in trying to answer. I don't do much worrying about what might have been.

McAleer: Rex Stout kept a record of his writing schedule. Do you keep a such record?

Cain: I don't keep any journal, and in fact, when a story is done it passes out of my mind completely. I've come across scripts which for one reason or another seem not to have gone to the agent—and read them with complete bewilderment, having no recollection whatever of the idea, the writing, or anything about them. In a way, this is a mercy, as you could go nuts thinking old ideas over. In fact, as I've already mentioned, Hemingway was close to setting himself nuts over what was said about him, and in that way let his old books possess him, where he shouldn't have—or at least, say I would feel that I shouldn't.

McAleer: Do authors need literary agents?

Cain: They are a very important part of a writer's life. You write a novel, then send it to the agent, and he takes over the selling of it, collecting the money for it, selling it abroad, and all the rest—or in my case, she does. I think most critics are ignorant of this aspect of a writer's career, but they shouldn't be. A good agent will make the difference between success or failure for many a writer.

[Compiler's note: Cain died 27 October 1977, two years to the day after Stout.]

NOTE FROM THE COMPILER

I received an odd e-mail in July of 2009. The note said simply, "Are you the Harry Sapienza who interviewed James Cain back in the 1970s?" I noted that the email indicated it was sent from an amcaleer. Well, of course I was the Harry Sapienza who interviewed him—I mean, how many people could possibly end up with that unlikely name? In any case, I had done it, enjoyed it, and hadn't thought about it in a long time. So, naturally I wrote back confirming and asking why he wanted to know.

Andy has explained in his introductory comments how he stumbled upon the work his father had done so long ago. I was surprised and pleased that he asked me to say a little about my tiny role in this project. The details of my interviewing Mr. Cain are spotty on most points but distinct on some others. Yet he made a clear impression upon me that lingers and that reminds me of the differences in the times then and now.

If you look up James M. Cain on Wikipedia, you will find that it says that he lived the majority of the end of his life in University Park, Maryland. He died October 27, 1977. His fourth wife had died in 1966. I was lucky enough to interview him in November of 1975. The house I went to, though, was in Hyattsville, Maryland—not the ritzier neighborhood of University Park. Cain, I found, was simpler and humbler than I had imagined. It was a quiet two hours that I still remember.

I walked up the concrete path to the house at the address I had for Cain. The day was drizzly and dull, and the neighborhood decidedly ordinary and familiar. Nothing especially caught the eye about this house or this yard. Well, what did I expect, I thought?

An elderly man answered the door, fairly trim and slightly bent. I introduced myself, and Mr. Cain invited me in. He had been expecting me.

The interior of the house was as simple, modest, tasteful and unremarkable as the outside of the house. He had a small living room, the curtains were partially closed, and the room was lit primarily by a small lamp on a coffee table next to the couch. Mr. Cain offered me tea, which I accepted. We sat sipping the tea, primarily in silence. I think I may have asked Mr. Cain how long he had lived there, and I told him that I had spent a good deal of time nearby as I had gone to junior high in the area and had played in marching band from the area.

It was clear that Mr. Cain was not necessarily interested in small talk, and we got right down to my asking him about his years in Hollywood. As you have the transcripts, I will not repeat much of what was said, but will give my impression of his story. I tried to speak as little as possible and to let him tell me what he thought without interruption, which I sensed fit his preferences.

I guess that what struck me most was the straightforward, matter-of-fact humility in his reflections on his times as a "star" screenwriter. He had gone to Hollywood, it seemed, not with a sense of awe or of importance but of simply doing what he needed to do to pursue his career. I wouldn't say that his success surprised him; rather, it seemed that he saw no reason to make the fuss over it that others apparently made of it. Mr. Cain was not impressed with Hollywood executives, the studios, or the trappings. Nor did he seem to particularly enjoy being out there. He seemed to feel out of place, a simple guy in a glitzy place that he didn't buy into.

The one part of the conversation that did seem to warm his heart and animate his conversation was when he talked about the "triangle girls" who populated and enlivened the studio area for him. As you will see from the interviews, Cain described Marilyn Monroe as a typical triangle girl, at least before fame and fortune transformed everything for her. Like so many of his characters, these young women seemed to be the kind of salt-of-the-earth, common "girls" out to make their way in the world, catch or make their own break—simultaneously innocent and jaded, street-smart and naive. Marilyn famously rose above the rest, soaring like Icarus until the inevitable crash came. Cain knew her when she was young and striving. He liked her; he liked her type—all of them for their common charm and their obvious charms.

Beyond these memories, it seemed to me that these were not happy times for Cain. He found it hard, I think, to write screenplays. It simply wasn't the genre he was geared toward, and he did not seem to fit into the social structure nor the "artistic" climate. He didn't say it in so many words, but Cain seemed to truly deplore the falseness—not just of Hollywood and its obsession with commercialism—but equally the pretenses of some successful writers.

Cain did not talk about his own marriages, his parents, or his dreams. He talked about writing, and he talked about the studios and the pressures of working to find solely toward commercial success. He seemed to imply that his earlier successes occurred because he did not try to write them for Hollywood. His professional career involved his early reporting, his early novel writing, his Hollywood years, and his later more obscure period. Of these, the Hollywood years were remembered least fondly.

As Mr. Cain continued to speak, I completely forgot that I was listening to someone once considered a significant "celebrity." He never attempted to impress me in any way—with his accomplishments or with the cleverness and depth of his knowledge of writing. He marched with me through the questions, simply and deliberately. Finally, everything that I had come to ask had been asked and answered. He uttered his final "What else you got?" and I thought, I got nothing. But now, I realize, I was wrong.

A curious set of circumstances led me to the door of James M. Cain the day after Thanksgiving, 1975. I had moved up to Boston in January and took a job at what was then Mt. Ida College in Needham. It was a sudden break to get the job, and I realized I needed to acquire a Masters degree. My plan was to enter UMass-Boston as quickly as possible. My intent was to major in 19th century American literature—as I was a huge fan of Poe, Hawthorne, and Melville. There were no summer courses available at UMass, but there was a Chaucer course at Boston College. So, I thought, well, I may as well take something during the summer. Long story short is that the course was taught by Dr. Charlie Regan, a charismatic and humorous mediaevalist, who talked me into applying to Boston College, instead, and majoring in mediaeval literature, instead. He also suggested that a research assistantship would familiarize me with graduate life. The mediaeval English department was tiny, however and had no assistantships available, so I was assigned to Dr. John McAleer.

Professor McAleer was working on a biography of James M. Cain, he told me. Had I heard of Cain? I thought I might have. Was I familiar with *The Postman Always Rings Twice* and *Double Indemnity*? I guess I'd seen them, I said, but hadn't read either. Well, it didn't matter, he said. All he wanted me to do for the moment was to proofread the Introduction he was writing. So I started working for Dr. McAleer. We'd get together every couple of weeks to go over what he had written. He was incredibly kind about my impertinent corrections.

Somewhere along the line in these conversations I mentioned to Dr. McAleer that I was going back home for Thanksgiving. What electrified him was when I told him that "home" was Takoma Park, Maryland. This is fantastic, he said. Would I be willing to interview Cain for him? I hesitated, thinking of how my "vacation" might now be spent. He said he wanted to ask Cain about his Hollywood years. Now I was intrigued and immediately agreed. And the rest as they say, "Is history." Now, if we had e-mail back in 1975 would Professor McAleer have had to assign me the Cain Q&A? I don't like to think about it.

–Harry Sapienza, Ph.D.
University of Minnesota

AFTERWORD: WHAT ELSE YOU GOT?

If you've read this far, I'm going to assume that you enjoyed the foregoing interviews with James M. Cain, as I did. So let's devote this short afterword to what we can learn from his comments.

To me, the catch-phrase Cain used after nearly every string of interview questions ("What else you got?") is the best description of his own writing: direct on the one hand and spare on the other. No fooling around, no elaborate qualifying clauses. I think Cain envisioned the novel as the story of a character told through dialogue. My nominee as best current practitioner of this approach would be Elmore Leonard, who also provided an epigraph or two for this wonderful project by the McAleers.

Some examples to illustrate my theory:

In Chapter 1, Cain says that he never believed that his experiences a journalist helped him in writing fiction. I'd argue that this is because most articles by reporters are necessarily in the third-person form of narrative, while Cain truly felt that "to write a novel, I have to pretend to be somebody else ... the character telling his story." I think that's why Cain preferred first-person narrative to the third-person one for fiction, though he did produce three books in the latter form.

Also in Chapter 1, Cain makes a point about profanity or vulgarity in dialogue that I've often impressed upon my writing students: "[I] sometimes use a ... LITTLE profanity ... , but it's like garlic: A little bit goes a long way." My version of this view is that you don't want your dialogue to "be" natural, you want it to "sound" natural. The difference?: In the real world, a street-level drug dealer might use the "f---" word ten times in one paragraph of speech as verb and noun, adjective and adverb. But, if you have a fictional character who's supposed to be a street-level drug dealer, the "f---" word can and should be injected only occasionally so that character "sounds" natural, allowing the reader to subliminally supply the remainder of the real-world profanity without avalanching the audience with that character "being" natural.

Finally, and again in Chapter 1, Cain is asked about the ethnic prejudices expressed or displayed by many of the characters in his novels. He replies, "[The slurs don't] say that I [the author] have any ethnic prejudice, it says the character [does]." This reminds me of another lesson I try to drive home in my seminars: Your characters don't have to be "politically correct" as fictional speakers, but you do have to be "demographically accurate" as an author of sequential novels. For example, in many parts of the United States, the organized crime families have predominantly been immigrants from Italy or Italian-Americans born here. Therefore, to be "demographically accurate," you may have to cast Italian-American characters in such roles. However, while many or even all your mob characters might be Italian-

American, you should not have all your Italian-American characters be mobsters in sequential novels. In that next book, make your homicide detective or corporate lawyer or clinical psychologist Italian-American, because these roles, too, are "demographically accurate" and will create a more diverse cast for your readers to experience.

Cain also believed strongly in what I advocate as the principal tenet of the professional author: editing his own work. At the end of Chapter 3, he says, "I do a lot of rewrite, crossing out and tuning things up—that goes on all the time with me." I think this might be James M.Cain's greatest message to the rest of us: Great novels aren't written, they're re-written.

Now, if only I could remember the interview in which I first saw THAT quote.

Jeremiah Healy, aka "Terry Devane"
Boston, Massachusetts
www.jeremiahhealy.com

LaVergne, TN USA
07 March 2011
219229LV00004B/28/P